D1713537

# *Art in Action*

## *Have You Got What It Takes to Be an Animator?*

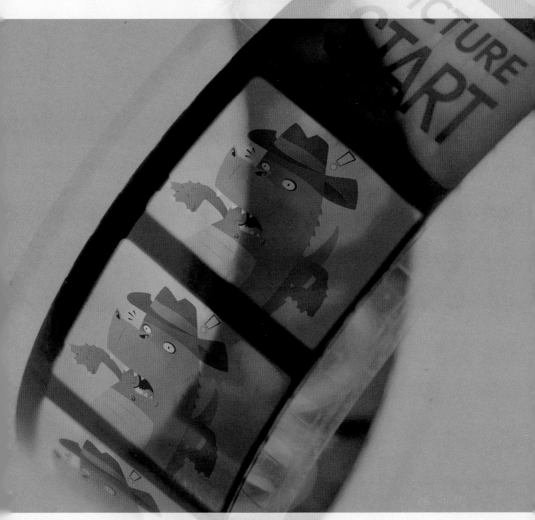

by Lisa Thompson

Compass Point Books ✦ Minneapolis, Minnesota

First American edition published in 2008 by
Compass Point Books
3109 West 50th Street, #115
Minneapolis, MN 55410

Editor: Mari Bolte
Designer: Lori Bye
Creative Director: Keith Griffin
Editorial Director: Nick Healy
Managing Editor: Catherine Neitge
Content Adviser: Larry Lauria, Animator/ Instructor,
                 Island Animation, Savannah, Ga.

Editor's note: To best explain careers to readers, the author has
created composite characters based on extensive interviews and research.

 This book was manufactured with paper containing
at least 10 percent post-consumer waste.
Printed in the United States of America.

Library of Congress Cataloging-in-Publication Data
Thompson, Lisa, 1969–
  Art in action : have you got what it takes to be an animator? / by Lisa Thompson.
  p. cm. — (On the job)
  Includes index.
  ISBN 978-0-7565-3623-7 (library binding)
  1. Animated films—Vocational guidance—Juvenile literature.
  2. Animators—Juvenile literature. I. Title. II. Series.
  NC1765.T497 2008
  791.43'34023—dc22                           2007032706

Visit Compass Point Books on the Internet at *www.compasspointbooks.com*
or e-mail your request to *custserv@compasspointbooks.com*

# *Table of Contents*

# And ... Action!

I can sense my team's excitement as we gather for our first meeting about a new animation project. Andy, the director of a new short film, has brought us together to talk through the story so we have a clear picture of the movie he wants to make.

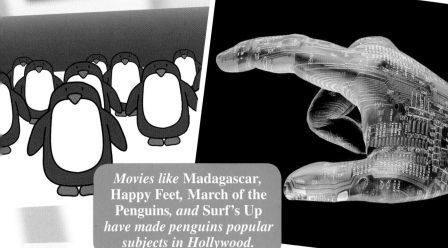

*Movies like* Madagascar, **Happy Feet, March of the Penguins,** *and* **Surf's Up** *have made penguins popular subjects in Hollywood.*

As their sequence director, I have the job of making sure my team of five animators stays on creative track and on schedule. The team has read the script, and we are now looking at the storyboard drawings pinned to the walls. Some of the team members have begun making small sketches of characters and key scenes they'd like to do.

It's an exciting time, and I can't help but feel nervous. My team and I normally work on creating animation for TV commercials or documentaries. The process of creating the movie won't be that different—but of course we'll have a lot more work to do.

Questions such as "How will those scenes be created?" and "What kind of techniques will we need to use?" are asked as my team tries to figure out the best way to bring the story to life.

Louie - Tracking Shot

more *speed* desperate

close-up - Bish catches up

Louie. gasping, swiping?

Bish Extreme C-up

Hurrah! add cheering

The animation process is a lot of work, and we need to make sure we do everything to make the director's vision possible. In the end, though, it's a rewarding experience to see your hard work come to life!

The director goes through the story and explains how he imagines the finished film will look. We talk about the characters— their personalities, unique traits, motives, the places they visit, the world they live in, and other important tidbits. Then we look at the colors, lighting, and camera angles for each scene.

There are lots of questions—the team wants as much information as possible so we can understand Andy's vision for the film. We leave the meeting feeling inspired and excited, armed with a lot of notes and clear ideas about the look and feel of the film.

It's my job to assign key scenes and characters to each of my animators. Some of my team have already told me what they would like to work on. I warn them that I won't be bribed with candy bars (unless they are caramel-filled!), and I sit down to decide who will be working on what.

# Animation techniques

## 2-D cel animation

This is the most traditional form of animation. It involves sketching a picture by hand, turning the page, and drawing the same picture in a slightly different position. The sketches are outlined in ink, filled in with color, and shot on film. An animator can also scan drawings into the computer to turn pencil lines into black, inked lines. Then, with a point of the cursor and a click of the mouse, the areas are filled in with color.

## Stop-motion animation

This technique involves building small models, photographing them, slightly moving the characters, and then photographing them again. It takes a lot of patience, since 24 pictures create just one second of film or video. It can take 20 minutes to set up each shot. Tim Burton's *The Nightmare Before Christmas* took three years to complete—the scenes took so long to set up that one week's worth of shooting equaled just one minute of film.

## CGI (computer-generated imagery)

This involves sculpting shapes called polygons on the computer to build the characters and sets. Modelers make CG models of the characters. Animators move the characters. Other artists add textures, lighting, and effects. The result is a 3-D image that can be manipulated to be seen from any angle.

# Who's Who on the Team?

Putting an animation project together is a team effort, even though every member of the team usually works independently toward the common goal.

In small productions, animators may take on more than one role—in fact, they might take them all on!

The key roles when putting an animation together are:

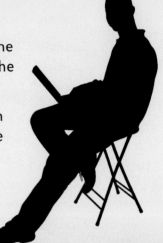

## Writer

Writers create the story and script for the animation. Writing for animation requires paying special attention to creating characters, scenes, and settings that will work well visually.

## Director

The director is the creative leader of the film. He or she guides the whole team and ensures that everyone knows the style and type of story that they are trying to tell, as well as what the result should be.

## Art director

The art director is responsible for the look of the animation. His or her job is to find the best possible way to tell the story. Good art direction always supports and reinforces the aims of the story and the characters.

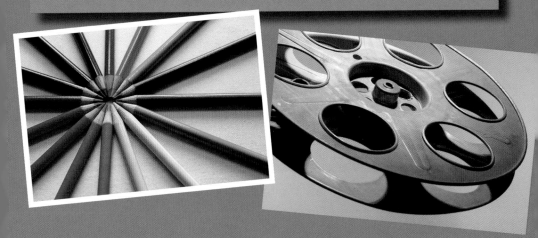

## Producer

The producer is the business leader of the film. It is his or her job to take care of budgets, schedules, and contracts, as well as making sure the creative team is meeting all of its deadlines. The producer works closely with the director to keep the project on time and within the budget.

## Illustrator/storyboard artist

To begin turning a story into animation, illustrators draw sketches to show the look and feel of the story. They develop key characters and action sequences with scenes so the plot can come to life visually.

Storyboard artists work with the director to break the story into a series of scenes. They create storyboards that visually show how the scenes flow together, so everyone involved understands how the finished animation will look.

## What is a storyboard?

A storyboard is a group of sketches, arranged in order, that show the scenes and action changes for an animation. They are used for movies, TV shows, and even advertisements.

## Editor

Editors work with the director to make sure the images, timing, and sound of the final animation work well together.

## Composer and sound director

Composers are responsible for all the music in an animation. They work closely with the sound director, who arranges all the needed sound effects, such as slamming doors and footsteps.

# Computer graphic artist

Computer graphic artists build computer-generated versions of the characters and settings. Some artists may specialize in just one area, such as lighting.

## The stages of CGI animation

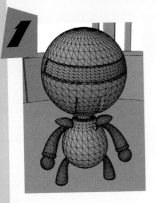

1. Modelers create the outside models of the characters. Riggers rig the inside skeletons of the characters to set their range of movement.

2. Animators bring the characters to life, acting out the script and storyboard.

3. Technical directors apply the textures and lighting.

4. Effects animators work on rain, wind, lightning, snow, and other forces of nature.

# How I Became an Animator

For as long as I can remember, I've loved drawing funny characters and making up stories about them. When I was 5, I created a whole town of thumbprint characters and pages of comic-strip adventures about them. There was even a superhero, Thumbman, and his friend, Princess Pinkie. Hey, you've got to start somewhere!

This is my brother!

This is Emerald the fish.

I was forever trying to squeeze in time to watch one more cartoon on TV before I went to school each morning. I'd save up my pocket money so I could see any new animated movie as soon as it came out.

I still remember the first time I saw *The Little Mermaid*. I was drawn into the world on the screen, and the characters felt real to me. I loved the power of the story and its color and energy. It was then that I knew I wanted to create characters that would come alive on the screen.

From around the age of 8, I started writing stories and keeping folders to hold all the characters I created. Sure, the stories and characters never really got much further than the folders (some never even made it that far), but creating them got my imagination working.

**PUN FUN**

Animators always know where to draw the line.

I developed ideas and a passion for writing good stories. It helped me understand what makes a good animated story, and it honed my drawing skills. Creating those folders started me on the road to becoming an animator.

He waits...

Deep in thought.

a voice calls out...

someone needs him!

Thumb Man to the Rescue

He's coming!!

THUMBMAN.

A. option

B.

C. option

A. option

B. option

PRINCESS MURIE

C. option

D. option

BOING

As I got older, I became interested in computers and began creating short animated clips on my computer. I'd scan in my drawings and then add color and sound. In creating these little two- to five-minute animated films, I learned the basics of animation and how to use the computer software.

*Starting early is an advantage for an animator.*

After I left school, I went to college, where I studied art and animation. My coursework included hands-on experience. I got to work at several companies, creating animations for the Web, computer games, commercials, and films. On top of studying, that made for a busy time!

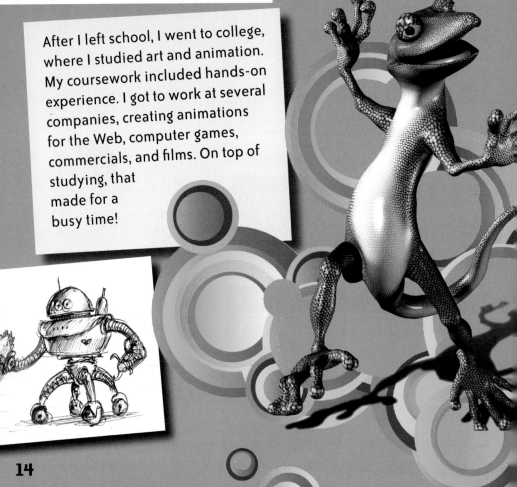

I was lucky enough to work with modelers, writers, directors, and producers. They helped me understand what it is like to be part of a creative team—bouncing ideas off each other and coming up with new ways of doing things.

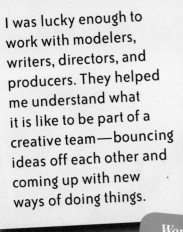

*Working closely in a team gives you support and inspiration.*

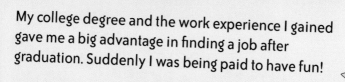

My college degree and the work experience I gained gave me a big advantage in finding a job after graduation. Suddenly I was being paid to have fun!

Most of the animation I create now is done on computers. However, I still like drawing my little characters in pencil and creating funny stories about the thumb people. One day I might even find the time to do an animated movie about them—*The Adventures of Thumb Town.* Now that's a great story!

# A Good Animator ...

- Can draw well and has a flair for art

- Has an active imagination

- Understands how stories work

- Has an eye for detail

- Works well with computers

- Thinks creatively in both two dimensions and three dimensions

- Is a visual problem solver

- Can make deadlines

- Is prepared to do painstakingly detailed work

- Can work both independently and as part of a team

- Likes to keep learning (advances in animation software are constant)

- Is an actor—a real ham!

**PUN FUN**  Animators are colorful people who draw on their emotions.

— ORIGIN 1950s:

**animation** • n. 1

chiefly archaic

**Animation:** *noun*
1. animated quality; liveliness; spirit; life
2. the act of animating; the act of bringing to life
3. the process of creating animated cartoons

## Look around ... animation is everywhere!

### Video games

In 1997, Square Soft Inc. released the game *Final Fantasy VII*. The game contained more than 40 minutes of full-motion movies, 20 fully drawn computer-generated cities and towns to play in, and at least 50 hours of game play. It was the first role-playing game to offer seamless transitions from animated movie sequences to actual gameplay. The entire game was three-dimensional, with fully rendered characters on pre-drawn backgrounds.

### Science

In 2006, Harvard University chose the scientific animation company XVIVO to create an animation for its molecular and cellular biology program. The company created an eight-minute 3-D animation of the microscopic cellular world.

### Commercials

In 1999, the auto insurance company GEICO introduced its new mascot, a CGI lizard created by Framestore CFC, the largest digital-effects company in Europe. A team of 10 animators is responsible for making the gecko as realistic as possible.

## Other places you can find animation:

- **Entertainment**—movies, TV shows, videos, games, and documentaries
- **Manufacturing**—advertising, training videos, marketing, and promotion
- **Science**—teaching videos, research explanations, and research projections
- **Medicine**—research, training, and investigation
- **Architecture**—projections and design
- **Airlines**—flight investigation and pilot training
- **Sports**—on giant screens in stadiums during games

17

# The 3 Stages of Animation

1. PREPRODUCTION
2. PRODUCTION
3. POSTPRODUCTION

**These steps are followed to create CGI animation:**

Step 1

## PREPRODUCTION

1. Writers write the story in script form.

2. The script is read, discussed, and fine-tuned.

3. Illustrators draw sketches of scenes and characters.

4. Storyboard artists create hundreds of storyboard drawings to map out the story, scene by scene.

5. Characters' voices are recorded.

6. Character and background styles are chosen.

7. Storyboards are put into their final order and are timed with the characters' voices, rough music, and other sounds. Then this is shot on film or videotape, creating the story reel.

# PRODUCTION

8. From drawings, modelers create CG computer models of the characters, props, and sets.

9. Each computer model has a set of controls that determines how it will move. Dozens of character files for movement and facial features, or places where action will happen, are created.

10. Background sets are created in a rough, blocked-out form.

11. Technical directors add special textures, such as skin, fur, and hair.

12. Animators create specific key poses that dictate the movement and emotion of each character.

13. Special effects, like flowing water, lighting, shadows, weather elements, and fire, are added to backgrounds and characters.

14. Rough animation is finalized and approved by a director. A final 3-D "render," or version, of the animation is produced.

# POSTPRODUCTION

15. The many individual animated layers that make up each shot are combined to create the final scenes. This is called compositing.

16. Editors create the final version of the film, making sure color levels are correct for all scenes. Special effects are finalized, and any additional required effects are added.

17. Volume levels for music, sound effects, and dialogue are balanced for the best dramatic effect.

19

# Telling the Story

The first step for any animated film is getting the story right. Not all stories are suitable for animation. An animated story needs to have good visual potential, action, and conflict. Think about how the story would look in pictures.

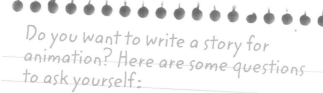

Do you want to write a story for animation? Here are some questions to ask yourself:

- What is the story about?

- How is the story told?

- Who is the hero?

- What does the hero want?

- Who or what is stopping the hero from getting what he or she wants?

- How does the hero achieve his or her goal (or not) in the end?

Things to remember
about being an animator:
Animation is time-consuming. There
are thousands of details involved in
every shot. Whether it's a tiny movement of the eyes or a slight ripple of
fur, an animator can tweak a single
shot for weeks!

Projects can last from just a few
days or weeks, when making an
advertisement, to months or even
years when making a feature film.
I enjoy this kind of project-based
work, since it means facing new
challenges on a regular basis.

## What's it about?

You need to understand what kind of story you are telling.
A story could have one or more of the following themes:

- Action
- Mystery
- Comedy
- Quest
- Thriller
- Adventure
- Romance
- Tragedy
- Science fiction

You also need to be clear about what is driving your story
forward. For example, is it:

- Looking for something?
- Returning home or being free?
- Breaking a spell?
- Seeking justice or revenge?
- Finding love?
- Stopping an evil villain?

Remember that a character is defined by his or her actions.

# From Story to Script to Storyboard

When a story is finalized, it is written in a script format. A script (or screenplay) contains the dialogue. It also describes the characters and their motivations, lists scene locations, and includes stage directions.

Using the script, character sketches are drawn to show the look, feel, color, lighting, and mood of each character. These model sheets show the characters from various angles. Animators can use these sheets as a guide when creating the characters on computers.

Stage directions make up part of a script.

Here's a character file—notice how we learn what he'll look like in various positions.

Hundreds of these drawings map out the story in a visual way to create the storyboards. These quick sketches help plan every shot and the action of the film.

## Storyboards—the animation map

A storyboard looks like a comic-book version of the final film. It shows all the shots and camera movements. It is the map that guides everyone through the production process. Artists and technicians must painstakingly produce every single frame in an animated film so they can get very detailed results.

Opening shot

taking

Zoom spots spider

Close-up o

Fangs come out

angry spid

Once the storyboards are approved, a workbook is assembled from the key drawings. A workbook page contains panels from the storyboards with camera angles, technical information, and descriptions of the action.

## From storyboards to story reels

An editor adds rough voice recordings and other sound to the storyboard frames to create a story reel. The story reel becomes a template for the final film—an early and incomplete version of the film that grows as more roughly animated scenes are added to it.

Story reels help in timing the story and identifying any areas that still need tweaking.

# Great Moments in Animation History

**1892:** Charles-Émile Reynaud screens the first animated film in Paris, France. The film, with about 500 frames, is shown on a device similar to a modern film projector.

**1906:** *Humorous Phases of Funny Faces* is drawn by J. Stuart Blackton. The silent cartoon is three minutes long and moves at 20 frames per second.

**1914:** Windsor McCay draws 10,000 images, mounts them on cardboard, and registers it as a film called *Gertie the Dinosaur*. The film became part of McCay's vaudeville act. McCay would stand in front of a projection screen and call Gertie. She would perform tricks such as drinking water and playing with a mastodon, and she would cry. At the end of the show, McCay would walk offstage and reappear as an animated figure in his own cartoon. The total film was five minutes long.

**1928:** *Steamboat Willie*, created by Walt Disney and Ub Iwerks and starring Mickey Mouse, is released. It is the first cartoon with a synchronized soundtrack.

**1937:** Walt Disney's *Snow White and the Seven Dwarfs* is released. At 83 minutes long, it is the first successful animated feature film, as well as the first to be filmed in Technicolor. It is the 10th highest grossing film of all time (and the highest grossing animated film) in the United States, after adjusting for inflation. The movie wasn't released on video until 1994.

**1960s:** The production company Hanna-Barbera becomes the first animation studio to successfully create cartoons for television. Popular shows included *The Jetsons*, *The Yogi Bear Show*, *The Flintstones*, *Jonny Quest*, *Scooby-Doo, Where Are You!*, and *The Smurfs*.

**1987:** Matt Groening's cartoon *The Simpsons* first appears on the *Tracey Ullman Show*. In May 2007, the show reached its 400th episode at the end of its 18th season, making it the longest-running sitcom and animated show. In 2007, *The Simpsons Movie* set the record ($74 million) for the highest grossing opening weekend for a film based on a television series.

**1991:** Walt Disney's *Beauty and the Beast* is the first animated film to receive an Academy Award nomination for Best Picture.

**1995:** Pixar Animation Studios releases *Toy Story*, the first feature-length computer-animated film. John Lasseter, founder of Pixar, was given a Special Achievement Academy Award in 1996 for directing the movie. Animators worked more than 800,000 hours on the film.

**2001:** *Shrek* becomes the first movie to win an Academy Award for Best Animated Feature.

**2002:** Hayao Miyazaki's *Spirited Away* is the first anime film to win an Academy Award.

**2007:** Dreamworks Animation's *Shrek 3* sets the record for highest grossing animated film on its first weekend. The former record was set by *Shrek 2*.

GERTIE JUST LOVES AN A

BOX OFFICE

Released th

WILLIAM FOX

OFFICE ATTRACT

EXCHANGES IN ALL PRINCIPAL CITIES

# BREAKING THE STORY DOWN

The film is broken down into a series of sequences, or parts, such as the chase sequence, the fight sequence, and the party sequence. Each sequence contains several scenes.

A scene is a continuous block of storytelling that either is set in a single place or follows a character. The end of a scene is typically marked by a change in location or time.

A few seconds of animation contains hundreds or thousands of moving images and special features. An animator usually uses a special collection of colors for each scene, sequence, and character. These are called color keys.

## Get ready for some math

To make an animation come to life, each second of film has 24 individual frames.

Every action must be timed to look real and believable, so it is broken down into stages, such as standing, sliding, falling, landing, recovering, and standing up again. If this action is to last five seconds, 120 frames are needed (five seconds times 24). A 90-minute movie needs 129,600 frames.

The director and the artists work out a series of rough drawings (the storyboards) that illustrate how every scene in a sequence will look. These drawings determine what we see, camera angles, zooms in or out, and lighting.

After the storyboards are finalized, the director works with our layout artists to generate a CGI story reel of the film. This allows much more precise planning for special camera angles and lighting.

## Animation around the world

A distinctive type of Japanese animation is called anime. Often inspired by Japanese *manga* (comics), these animations have a strong visual style. They are used on television, in DVDs, and even in computer and video games.

*A manga-style drawing*

# Creating Characters

When a character's look is decided upon, a file is created that contains drawings of the character's eyes, body, and facial expressions. A single character may have hundreds of files of its features.

In traditional, hand-drawn animation, the animator sketches key poses—places where the character starts, stops, or changes direction. Assistant animators do the drawings in between the key poses.

In stop-motion animation, the animator moves and shoots the character in sequence, one motion after another.

In CGI animation, the animator sets key frames—much like the key poses of traditional animation. The computer fills in the motion between the key frames.

## Character tests

Before starting to create a character, an animator usually tests the model with some simple movement tests, such as a walk, a lip-synch test (to make sure mouth movements match speech), and an extreme-pose test. This is to see where the character needs improvement and what changes are needed to allow movement.

As an animator, I need to be good at interpreting body language. Character animators are often thought of as the actors of animated film. It is my job to combine body movement and facial expressions to give each character an individual personality.

Much of what we think and feel is communicated through our eyes, hands, how we move, and the way we use our bodies. Certain body movements, gestures, thinking time, and facial expressions show certain feelings and meanings.

*What do you suppose he's thinking?*

Before we begin to animate, the characters' voices are recorded. It is important to do this early in the process, so we can hear what each character sounds like. This will influence how we create the finer details of each character's look, behavior, and gestures.

The voice-over artist experiments with many voices and accents before the director decides on the right sound for each character.

A character's voice is so important that casting agents spend a lot of time getting the right actors for an animation. Famous actors often work in animated films to provide memorable voices, like Mike Myers' for the ogre in *Shrek*.

Getting a character's mouth to move in time with the voice-over of the dialogue is also important. Certain sounds need certain mouth shapes. Speech is broken down, frame by frame, into key sounds so that the mouth shapes can be defined.

**PUN FUN** Sometimes animators need to get in the right frame of mind.

The animator must place the correct mouth shape at the right point in the animation so the character seems to be making the right sound.

Once all the mouth shapes have been created, they are placed in the character's file library.

## Mouth positions

Here are a few examples of mouth positions you will recognize:

| mouth | | sound |
|---|---|---|
| lips pressed together | | mmm |
| lips come together to make a small circle | | oooo |
| mouth is open | | ahhhh |

# The Story Behind The Lion King

Most people know that when *The Lion King* was released in 1994, the movie was an instant success—but what you might not know is that the story didn't come easily at all. Quite a few years earlier, there was just a vague idea to make a film about lions because one of the producers thought lions were cool.

Disney's writers tried various storylines, and Disney artists created countless drawings of lions. They ended up with a story for a film called *King of the Beasts*. It was about a war between lions and baboons. Since Disney was already doing an animated film called *Beauty and the Beast*, the film was retitled *King of the Jungle*.

The problem was that lions live in the savannah, or open grasslands—not the jungle. For the next few years, many story drafts went in the trash because no one could quite figure out what the story was about.

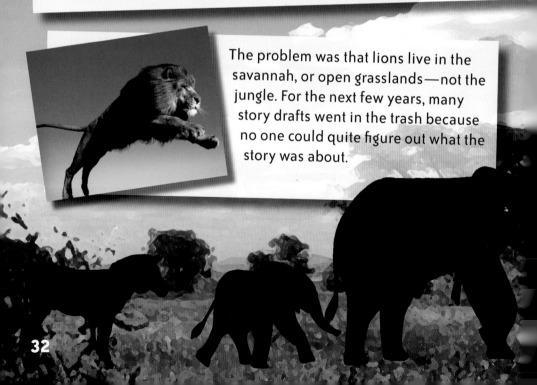

Eventually a team of writers and animators took a trip to Africa. The trip was an inspiration and provided many ideas that made it into the final movie. When the team got back, they worked solidly for two weeks with the producer and the co-director.

They looked at all the information they had collected. They took the story apart and figured out exactly who the characters were, what they wanted, and what action would drive the story.

Three years later, *The Lion King* finally reached the theaters. It became a smash hit around the world and proved how a little idea can become a great story if you don't give up and if you ask the right questions!

# Tricks of the Trade

## Distance from the camera

Certain types of shots give the viewer certain types of information:

- Long shots show large amounts of information and set the scene.

- Medium shots bring you into the action.

- Close-ups and extreme close-ups are good for showing emotion.

long shot

medium shot

close-up

## Camera angles

Camera angles influence how we understand a film. A weak character is often shown from a higher angle to emphasize his or her insignificance or smallness. In the same way, a tough, heroic character is often shown from below to make him or her appear big and strong. A wide frame, with not much in it, can make a character appear isolated or lonely.

## Lens lingo

Film professionals describe camera movements with special terms, including:

- **Trucking in**—camera moves toward an object

- **Panning**—camera moves from side to side

- **Tilting**—camera lens swings up or down

- **Dolly shot**—whole camera moves up or down

## Editing magic

### Timing

A lingering camera shot allows us to connect emotionally with characters, while fast cuts, or jumps to a new shot, force us to constantly reassess the situation. Compare the average length of shots in a fight or action sequence with those in an emotional scene. You'll find action shots are short and snappy, and emotional scenes use fewer and longer shots.

### Image sequence

The way images are arranged tells us about settings and emotions. Editors can put shots into an order different from that of the storyboard, or even cut out whole sequences. Such editing can change not only the feel of the story, but also the story itself.

In animation, the editor makes the most extreme cuts early, at the story reel stage. Otherwise animators could waste time creating something that would just end up on the cutting-room floor.

**PUN FUN**

When the animator tried to draw a cube, he had a mental block.

## Motion capture

In motion capture (called mo-cap), optical or magnetic markers are placed on an actor's major joints. The actor performs the desired movements while wearing these markers. The movement of the markers is recorded for storage in a computer.

The recorded motion of the actor's joints is mapped onto the computer-generated character's joints. This means the animated character is a combination of the movements of the actor and the CG character.

The makers of computer and video games are the biggest users of mo-cap. The technique helps them create realistic characters for their games.

# Special effects

Almost all movies we see today have some kind of CG special effect in them. It might make a natural element like fire, smoke, or clouds look more dangerous, or add a character or background. The character Jar Jar Binks in Episodes 1 to 3 of *Star Wars* was almost completely computer generated. His appearance was the first time such a detailed CG character interacted with live actors in a motion picture.

Special-effects animators often use computer programs to re-create the look and motion of real things. Examples are clouds swirling and a rock falling and bouncing.

That lets them see where and when to add enhancements or even a completely different effect. For instance, a flash of light or puff of smoke might not naturally occur but would look believable.

*Computer programs calculate how to make animated water ripples look realistic.*

# Behind the Scenes

### After the meeting

Many caramel-filled candy bars later, I gather my team to let them know what characters and scenes they will be working on. I give each animator a scene list, one major character, and one or two minor characters.

My major character is a crocodile named Louie, and my minor characters are a pair of swamp flies called Bisk and Ed. Time to do some research!

I create model sheets for each character, so I have a quick-reference guide showing its basic expressions, like happy, surprised, normal, scared, and excited.

After all the characters are modeled and their texture has been applied, I run through movement sequences with each one.

*One of Louie's model sheets*

LOUIE
THE CROC

All the while, we must follow the technical specifications of each scene and setting as outlined in the workbook.

I play around with Louie, trying to get his personality and little unique traits just right. I pay particular attention to his eyes, snout, and tail.

They're starting to look good!

I LIKE THIS FLY. I'LL WORK ON THIS ONE.

IDEAS OF SWAMP FLIES

I do the same with Bisk and Ed. It is important to experiment with all the characters until you know how they would look and react in any situation. Try to know the character as well as you know a member of your own family.

Now that we all know our characters and scenes, we get to work to bring them to life. Over the next several months, we will work with the art director, modelers, and technical directors to choose colors for characters and scenes, apply texture, and create character files.

## The Sweatbox

Every day, each animator shows Andy, the director, his or her play blasts. These are low-resolution versions of his or her work. A play blast can contain anything from a group of key character frames to an almost completed scene. The editors then add the sound to all the play blasts and place them into the story reel.

The team, along with Andy, views the work to see where we've gotten and whether anything needs changing. This step in the process is often called The Sweatbox because it is a tense time for animators.

Piece by piece, the animation comes together. The studio becomes a busy hive of activity as we work hard to create our characters and scenes, hoping to stay on top of our deadlines!

## Time to flip

A flip book contains a series of pictures that change gradually from one page to the next. When you turn the pages quickly, the pictures appear to move, creating animation. There are software packages and Web sites that convert digital video files into custom-made computer flip books.

The deadline draws near.

Every Friday the editors put the whole week's work together into the story reel. Then we have a screening so the entire team, which includes the director, producer, animators, and modelers, can see how it's looking.

Weeks turn into months. The days get longer and the nights get later as we rush to meet deadlines. We begin to talk about our characters as if they really do exist.

Each week the screenings get more and more exciting as the characters and scenes become more complete.

You have good days and bad days with your characters, just as if they were real. I chat with the other animators about my characters and what they're doing, and the other animators do the same.

I begin to realize that I am spending more time with Louie, Bisk, and Ed than I am with my real friends! It's getting weird, but I know the end is near.

### The final countdown

Some scenes are ready to have their special effects added and are almost complete.

Individually we show our work to Andy and the editor and make any final adjustments. At this point, we just need to tweak the lighting or add minor elements or props.

*It's almost time!*

Computers are perfect for something as time-consuming as animation. Now we can make changes in minutes that would take days to redraw by hand in traditional cel animation.

Finally we hand everything over to the postproduction team. All we can do now is wait.

**PUN FUN**
When animators dream in color, it's a pigment of their imagination.

# The Big Night

It's the moment of truth—we are finally going to see the result of all our hard work.

The lights go down, the music begins, and the world my team and I helped bring to life appears. Suddenly I see Louie race across the screen, with Bisk chasing close behind.

It's so exciting. I loved creating that scene. Everyone laughs as Bisk crosses the line first. My heart jumps with pride. One by one, the team members get to see their characters and scenes on the big screen.

Weeks of work flash by in seconds, months flash by in minutes. It's such a thrill for us to see how wonderful the animation looks and to know that we were able to achieve so much.

Even though we know the story inside and out, we don't even want to blink in case we miss a frame. It's like meeting with old friends—to us, our characters really have come to life!

# Follow These Steps to Become an Animator

At school, studying art, improving your drawing skills, and learning computer skills will start you in the right direction. A strong math foundation will also help with the technology side of the job.

A commitment to keep learning is essential for an animator. A college degree in animation, fine art, or media is best. The job is very technical, so this training is important. It is also a great way to get hands-on experience and to meet people in the industry.

When you start your animation career, remember that keeping up with developments in technology is fundamental to the job. Animation is not for those who don't like change!

Animation is time-consuming, and you will spend long periods in front of your computer monitor. You may need to work long hours to meet deadlines. But this kind of project-based work provides plenty of challenges and opportunities to learn, and the excitement of creating amazing animation!

# Finding work experience

Internships and other work experience will help you get your foot in the door. Combine that with an impressive design portfolio to demonstrate your drawing skills, and include a CD or DVD with examples of your animations.

## Opportunities for animators

### Many industries use animation. The job possibilities include:

- **Storyboard artist**—produces storyboards for film projects

- **Film animator**—animates for short films and feature-length movies

- **Game designer**—creates computer or video game animation

- **Visual-effects artist**—focuses on special-effects animation

- **Layout artist**—designs sets and environments for animated characters

- **Technical director**—designs textures and lighting for characters and sets

- **Art director**—establishes the look and color choices for a film

- **Broadcast graphic designer**—creates titles and animations for television stations

# Find Out More

## In the Know

- The movie *Transformers*, a combination of computer-generated characters and live action, set box office records in 10 countries when it was released in 2007. The movie's visual effects were so complex that each frame of movement took 38 hours to process.

- The animation company Pixar hosts an in-house professional-development program that offers more than 110 fine arts courses, including creative writing, sculpting, and drawing, to any Pixar employee.

- The U.S. Department of Labor estimates that the average pay for animators is about $28 an hour, or about $58,000 a year. The lowest 10 percent earn about $15 an hour, or about $30,000 a year, or less. The highest 10 percent earn about $45 an hour, or about $93,000 a year, or more.

## Further Reading

Hahn, Don. *Disney's Animation Kit Workbook*. New York: Disney Press, 1999.

*The History of Moviemaking: Animation and Live-Action, From Silent to Sound, Black-and-White to Color*. New York: Scholastic, 1995.

Parks, Peggy J. *Computer Animator.* Detroit: KidHaven Press, 2006.

Serkis, Andy. *The Lord of the Rings: Gollum: How We Made Movie Magic*. Boston: Houghton Mifflin, 2003.

## On the Web

For more information on this topic, use FactHound.

1. Go to *www.facthound.com*
2. Type in this book ID: 0756536235
3. Click on the *Fetch It* button.

# *Glossary*

**anime**—a style of animation originating in Japan

**camera angle**—where a camera is placed to make a shot

**cel**—hand-drawn sheet representing a single animation frame

**compositing**—combining images from more than one source to create the illusion that all the images are from the same scene

**computer-generated imagery (CGI)**—application of computer graphics to create special effects in films, TV commercials, and other media

**frame**—single photographic image bordered by frame lines and traditionally in strips contained in reels; 24 frames are in one second of film

**optical**—relating to light

**production**—process by which a film is created; something that is produced

**scene**—continuous block of storytelling, either in a single place or following a single character

**sequence**—continuous or connected series

**special effects**—effects used to produce scenes that cannot be achieved by normal or natural methods (especially on film)

**storyboard**—series of illustrations in sequence to visually show a story

**Technicolor**—film process widely used from the 1930s to the 1950s that had realistic, rich colors

**three-dimensional (3-D)**—having three dimensions: length, width, and depth

**trait**—distinguishing feature

**two-dimensional (2-D)**—having two dimensions: length and width; hand-drawn traditional animation is 2-D

**vaudeville**—popular theater entertainment in America from the 1880s to the 1920s, featuring music, comedy, magic, and acrobatics

**visual potential**—suitability for use in a visual format

**voice-over artist**—professional actor who provides the offscreen voice for characters or narration in media, such as television, film, and radio

# Index

## Look for More Books in This Series: